WELCOME TO

Beast
Quest

WITH

Collect the special coins in this book.
You will earn one gold coin for
every chapter you read.

Once you have finished all the chapters,
find out what to do with your gold coins at
the back of the book.

With special thanks to Tabitha Jones

For Andrew Jones

www.beastquest.co.uk

ORCHARD BOOKS
Carmelite House
50 Victoria Embankment
London EC4Y 0DZ

A Paperback Original
First published in Great Britain in 2015

Beast Quest is a registered trademark of Beast Quest Limited
Series created by Beast Quest Limited, London

A CIP catalogue record for this book is available from
the British Library.

ISBN 978 1 40833 495 9

1 3 5 7 9 10 8 6 4 2

Printed and bound by CPI Group (UK) Ltd, Croydon, CR0 4YY

The paper and board used in this book are made from wood
from responsible sources.

Orchard Books
An imprint of Hachette Children's Group
Part of The Watts Publishing Group Limited
An Hachette UK Company

www.hachette.co.uk

Beast Quest®

YAKORIX
THE ICE BEAR

BY ADAM BLADE

ORCHARD

CONTENTS

STORY ONE

The snow lies thickly on the ground and the cold wind howls across the Icy Plains. But I do not feel it. The fire of my magic keeps me warm.

In the distance, I see the smoke rising from chimneys. To think, all of those innocent people huddled beside their fires. They have no idea what is coming! My steps have brought me to the crater of this ancient volcano. A few drops of my potion should be enough to wake the Beast that sleeps inside. The people will cower before her claws and teeth, and I will march on her back into the city itself.

And who will dare to stand in my way? That fool Tom, no doubt, but even he is no match for the creature that now stirs...

Kensa the Sorceress

A WINTER WITH NO SPRING

Tom's icy fingers tingled as he stretched them towards the parlour fire. Outside, the wind was raging. Tom could hear it howling through chinks in the palace mortar as if Luna the Moon Wolf was trying to break in. He glanced towards the window. Leaden clouds were hurling more snow towards the already

smothered ground. *Is this storm ever
going to stop?* Tom wondered, leaning
closer to the blaze. He glanced
towards his friends on the bench
beside him. Daltec, Avantia's Wizard,
was gazing thoughtfully over the
rim of his teacup at the flames while
Elenna huddled inside her cloak

munching a slice of toast. Across from
their bench, King Hugo and Queen
Aroha were taking their breakfast
from a low table before the hearth.
Aduro, the former Wizard, sat close to
the fire, his eyes half closed and his
chin on his chest.

"More tea?" King Hugo asked,

turning towards the queen.

Aroha was almost lost inside a pile of thick woollen robes, but her green eyes sparkled. "If it isn't already frozen," she said. She let out a brittle laugh. "You know, Hugo, if I'd had any idea Avantian winters could be like this, I'd never have agreed to the wedding."

"If *I'd* known that Avantian winters could be like this," Hugo said, "I would have insisted we rule from your castle in Tangala."

Aroha smiled. "You'd never leave the people in their time of need," she said. Then she sat upright, her expression suddenly grave. "That reminds me," she said. "Captain Harkman told me this morning that the stockpiles of wood and grain we've been sending out to the villages are running low. If this winter goes on much longer, I don't know—"

The queen broke off as another icy gust swept across the room, making the candle flames dip and waver. Dark shadows reached up the parlour walls like gnarled fingers, and the endless screeching of the wind echoed in Tom's mind like evil laughter.

This terrible winter is bringing Avantia to its knees as surely as any Beast could, he thought. *But I can't fight the wind! Unless...*

Tom frowned, a dark thought taking shape in his mind. He turned to Daltec on the bench beside him.

"Daltec?" Tom said. "You've been

studying Avantia's weather records. Do you think this cold is natural? Or could there be a more sinister cause?"

Daltec tipped his head in thought, gnawing at his lip. Across the table, the king and queen waited, their faces etched with worry. "It's hard to say," Daltec answered at last. "The palace records do tell of hard winters in the kingdom's distant past. And weather is unpredictable…"

In his seat beside the fire, Aduro shook his head. "We have seen hard winters before, yes. But never like this. I had been hoping the weather would change, but now –" Aduro glanced at the bleak view through the window – "I fear Tom may be right."

King Hugo's frown deepened. "So

you think this weather is the work of one of Avantia's enemies?"

Aduro nodded. "I am starting to believe so, yes."

The queen gave a tired-sounding laugh. "Unfortunately that leaves us with rather a long list," she said. "Avantia has many foes."

Another gust of wind whirled through the chamber, snuffing out the candles and plunging them all into gloom. Tom heard a door bang shut below. He leapt from the bench as footsteps clattered up the stairs outside, accompanied by the sound of muffled voices.

"You need have no fear," Tom heard Captain Harkman say. "I said he'll see you and he'll see you. King Hugo turns no one away." There was a hurried rap at the door, and Captain Harkman entered followed by a man and a woman wrapped in threadbare cloaks. Their faces were pinched with hunger, and red-raw from the wind. As they turned towards the king, Tom noticed their eyes looked haunted and desperate.

"Your Majesty," the man said, bowing his head. "My name is Jerald, and I farm land up to the north in Yotai. Or at least, I used to. Now my fields are as hard as iron, and lie buried under snow. We cannot sow. We cannot farm. People will starve if there is no let-up in this storm."

The king nodded solemnly as the man spoke. Queen Aroha's gaze was filled with pity.

"Others have brought the same news to the palace," King Hugo said. "Even here in the south the fields are frozen. We are sending what aid we can, and I will do everything in my power to ease your suffering. But you must understand, even a king and his

Wizard cannot control the weather."
King Hugo spoke to his captain of
guards. "Harkman," he said, "please
take these two to the kitchens. Make
sure they get something hot to eat,
and ask Cook to give them a bundle
to take back to their village." King

Hugo turned to the farmer and his wife. "You may stay here until you are rested enough to return home." At the word "home", Tom saw Jerald's wife look up, her eyes wild with fear. She began to wring her hands.

"But what about the wild animal?" she blurted out. "I am afraid to return home while it roams free."

"Hush, Lara, hush," Jerald told his wife, taking her arm to guide her towards the door. Tom held up a hand.

"Wait," he said. "What animal? A wolf, or a bear of some kind?"

Lara shuddered violently and shook her head. "No bear I've ever seen," she said, her voice quivering with fear. "It's as tall as a tree and white like the snow, and has teeth as long as my arm. It's been trampling anything left in the fields and destroying our herds. As if we didn't have enough trouble finding something to eat. Folk are scared for their lives."

Jerald tugged at his wife's arm again. "Let's not bother the king and queen with foolish tales," he said. "It's just a bear, like the lad there said."

Tom shook his head. "No ordinary bear could cause so much destruction while Nanook protects the north."

Aduro nodded. "Tom is right," he said. "I feel Lara's tale is a clear sign that Evil is indeed at work."

Tom smiled grimly at the king and queen. "A Beast on the loose in the north?" he said. "I think that narrows our search down. And if Evil forces

are at work, they can be defeated."

Elenna was already on her feet at
Tom's side, her bow slung across her
back. "In that case, we'd better go,"
she said. "It sounds like an urgent
Quest awaits us."

1

A GOOD BEAST IN PERIL

Once Captain Harkman had led Jerald and his wife from the room, Daltec turned to Tom and Elenna. "How do we know that the Beast Lara describes isn't Nanook?" Daltec asked. "She could have wandered south towards the Central Plains now that the ice and snow has increased her range."

Elenna shook her head. "Nanook might frighten cattle by mistake, but she would never hurt them or trample crops. And she'd keep well away from towns."

"Then she must have come under some sort of evil enchantment," Daltec said. "There are no other Beasts in the North."

"Except one, perhaps," Queen Aroha said. "Ancient legends speak of an Ice Bear that roamed the North long ago – Yakorix, I think her name was. Wherever she walked, she brought winter in her path. What if those legends are true?"

"You're right, Aroha!" King Hugo said. "The story went that Yakorix fell into a volcano long before Avantian weather records began, taking her endless winter with her. I wonder if this confounded cold could mean that Yakorix was indeed a real creature, and has now escaped."

Elenna looked worried. "If a new Beast is prowling the North, Nanook must be in grave danger, otherwise she'd be protecting the people there."

Tom nodded, feeling a pang of anxiety for the Good Beast. "I have to contact Nanook," he said. "But she's too far away for me to speak to her through my red jewel...and even if I used the bell to summon her, she wouldn't be here for days..." Tom's voice trailed off. *What if I combine the two?* He took the red jewel from his belt.

"What are you doing, Tom?" Elenna asked, then her eyes widened. "You're going to merge their powers!"

Tom nodded. He held the red jewel against Nanook's brass bell, embedded in his shield.

Slowly, Tom's view of the king's

parlour was replaced by a mass of swirling white flakes. His ears rang with the angry raging of the wind. Tom looked down, and saw his body was covered in shaggy white fur. Nanook's fur. *I'm seeing through her eyes!* he realised. Suddenly, vicious pointed claws swiped towards him. *She's being attacked!* Nanook's paws flew up to block the blow, but the sharp claws snatched at her arm, leaving a row of bloody gashes. Nanook howled in pain, and charged towards the shadowy grey form that was attacking her. Tom tried to make out Nanook's attacker but caught only a glimpse of long, yellow fangs, dripping with saliva, and eyes that glowed yellow. The claws swiped again, and Nanook dodged, then lunged towards her assailant. Tom saw a shaggy fist flying towards him. *Watch out!* There was a thud, and his view seemed to lurch. Thick snow rushed up to meet him.

It took Tom a moment to realise that Nanook had fallen. He could hear her growling, the breath wheezing in her lungs. *You've got to get up!* There was a scuffling sound as Nanook heaved herself over, and Tom caught another glimpse of glowing yellow eyes, then the terrible curved claws slicing through the air. Nanook let out a bellow of pain and rage as the claws raked across her belly. *Nooo....*

Suddenly Tom felt something grip

his shoulder. He turned, and found himself back in the safety of the castle. Elenna was watching him, her eyes full of concern. "Are you okay?" she asked. "You were shuddering." Tom shook his head, trying to clear away the horror of the vision.

"Nanook has been attacked!" he said, his breath quick from worry. "We need to head north, now!"

Tom nodded to Aduro then bowed to the king and queen. "We're going north, Your Majesties. We need to help Nanook. Something's out there. Something evil."

King Hugo stared at Tom, his jaw clenched. "Of course. My people rely on you once again, Tom. Good luck, both of you."

There was no time to spare. Tom raced to the door with Elenna at his side. Together they flew down the stairs and Tom flung open the door to the courtyard outside. An icy blast met him, but Tom ignored the sharp sting of the cold. There was only one way to get to the North quickly enough. His hand touched the phoenix talon in his shield. *Epos!* Tom called with his mind. *Avantia needs you!*

As Tom and Elenna struck out across the courtyard, surrounded by flurrying snowflakes, Tom heard Daltec's voice calling him back.

"Tom, stop! Wait!"

Tom spun around. "There's no time!" Tom shouted back, raising his voice to be heard over the storm. "Nanook could die if we don't reach her soon."

"I understand," Daltec cried. "But you won't be of much use to Nanook if you arrive half frozen."

The young Wizard lifted his hands. An orange glow spread out from where he stood, making the falling snowflakes fizzle away. Tom felt a rush of heat and something as light as a feather and as warm as a quilt landed over his shoulders. It was a black cloak, patterned with red and orange flames. Tom lifted a corner of the garment. It was smoother than the finest silk.

Elenna grinned, running her hands over the fabric of her own cloak.

"Amazing!" she said. "I haven't been this warm for ages."

Daltec nodded. "The flame cloak is endowed with magical powers to preserve the heat of your body," he told her. "It will keep you safely warm for a while, but not forever.

You must complete your Quest and return as quickly as you can. And do not remove the cloaks on any account. Your body can become dangerously cold without you even realising."

Tom pulled his new cloak more closely about him. "Thank you, Daltec," he said. As he spoke, he heard a familiar, high-pitched keening on the wind. He looked up, and through the ragged grey clouds and falling snow he could see a glittering golden light. A moment later the huge red form of Epos was swooping in to land, golden talons extended, and fiery wings flung back.

As the phoenix touched down, her flickering flames extinguished and she extended a shining wing for Tom and Elenna to take a seat.

Tom's heart beat with hope at the sight of the mighty Beast. He scrambled up onto Epos's soft, warm feathers and held out a hand to Elenna. She climbed up beside him. They both threw a wave to Daltec, who was already hurrying back inside, then held tight to the ruff of feathers at the base of Epos's neck.

Tom felt Epos's muscles flex. Her wings beat downwards: once, twice – then Tom's stomach lurched as the phoenix soared skywards. Freezing air swept past, stinging Tom's cheeks and making his eyes water.

Finally Epos's wing beats slowed,

then stopped. The Flame Bird
had found an updraught and
was soaring through the cold air.
Tom pushed himself upright. The
freezing wind buffeting against him
made him gasp. When he had caught

his breath, he looked down.

The snowstorm was thinning, and Tom could make out the land far below, transformed by its frozen blanket. The snow was so deep it lay banked against houses and walls, turning everyday objects into strange white humps. Fields lay like blank sheets of parchment, and trees were grey skeletons. The whiteness went on as far as the eye could see, and as they travelled, Tom could feel the chill in the air getting fiercer.

"Tom!" Elenna said, pointing towards the ground. "Look at those poor sheep!"

Tom could see a huddle of grey forms with their heads hung low to the ground and snow piled up against them on every side.

"If this goes on much longer the livestock will freeze," Elenna said.

Tom nodded gravely. "Nothing can withstand this cold for long," he said. "If we don't succeed on this Quest, everyone will perish!" The thought sent a rush of adrenaline through Tom's body, making his face burn despite the bitter wind and snatching his breath away. He was used to lives depending on him. But the sheer scale of the disaster they faced... It was almost too heavy a burden to bear.

Tom forced himself to draw one deep, icy breath after another. *We'll save Nanook*, he told himself. *We'll find the source of this cold. We'll defeat it. This is a Beast Quest like any other, and while there is blood in my veins I won't fail.*

"Tom!" Elenna's voice cut into his train of thought. "Epos is falling." Tom shook himself, and saw that Elenna was right. They were passing over the Icy Plains, and Epos had lost the updraught she'd been riding. Her massive wings beat the air, but the strokes were stiff and slow. They were losing height fast.

"She's too cold to fly!" Tom realised. He clutched his red jewel. *Land, Epos!* But before Epos could follow his instruction, Tom felt her huge body sag. Her head fell forwards, and her limp wings folded behind her, tugged upwards by the wind. *She's fainted!*

Tom's stomach was left far above them as they plummeted at deadly speed towards the snowy ground.

3

THE ICE MARAUDERS

Tom and Elenna clung tight to Epos's feathers as freezing air rushed past them, threatening to pull them from the phoenix's back. Tom gritted his teeth and reached for the talon in his shield. "Epos! Wake up!" he cried. The wind screamed in Tom's ears as they fell and his cloak flapped madly around him. They were only seconds

from crashing to the blue-white ground.

Suddenly Tom felt a flicker of sleepy thought from the unconscious Beast. Confusion. Exhaustion. Agonising cold.

EPOS, FLY! Tom screamed the words with his mind. He felt the Flame Bird's consciousness flare as she awoke fully. Then there was a jolt of panic, as Epos realised the danger.

Her giant wings opened and pounded at the air, but the ground was rushing up to meet them far too fast.

"Hold tight, Elenna!" Tom cried. "This is going to be a bumpy landing!"

Epos reached her long talons down towards the icy ground.

CRASH! The phoenix smashed down, throwing Tom and Elenna

forwards across her feathers. She skidded across the ice, pushing up a great mound of snow before her, then finally came to a stop. Tom and Elenna leapt down and ran to Epos's side. The Beast's fiery eye looked dull. She raised her head slowly, but then let it sink back onto the ice. She gave a gentle sigh, and her orange eye flickered shut.

"She'll die out here!" Elenna cried. "She needs warmth!"

Tom put his hand on the majestic creature's side, feeling that her feathers were as cold as the hilt of his sword. Her ribs were barely moving, and Tom could see the smoking tendrils of air from her nostrils getting fainter with each breath.

He looked around the pale, barren landscape, and swallowed hard. Elenna was right. Epos was dying. He needed to get her warm.

"Maybe if we use our cloaks, we can warm her?" Elenna said.

But Tom shook his head. "They would barely cover her wing tip, and they have no power to restore her strength. But perhaps if we combine their warmth with healing magic…" Tom pulled his shield from his back and tugged Epos's golden talon from its place. Then he shrugged off his magical cloak. Right away he gasped as an icy hand seemed to grab his chest and squeeze. He caught his breath, already shivering, and realised how serious Daltec's advice had been

– the cloaks were vital to keeping them warm. Thankfully Tom also had Nanook's bell to offer him some protection from the terrible cold. Tom quickly wrapped Epos's talon in the silky fabric of his cloak, then held his shield up against the wind, blocking its deadly chill with the magic of Nanook's bell. He hoped that by combining the magical powers, he would revive the Flame Bird.

With his free hand, Tom held the cloak and healing talon up close to Epos's chest. Elenna stood by his side, watching the great Beast for any sign of life. Tom waited, willing her to breathe, but the Flame Bird's chest stayed still and silent. *Have I killed her?* Tom thought, a sickening

dread growing in his belly. But then
the feathers before him shifted as
Epos took a breath. And another.
The movement became stronger,
more insistent, and soon Tom could
feel a faint warmth coming from the
feathers on Epos's side as their golden
glow crept back.

"Epos!" Tom called. "Wake up!"
The creature's huge orange eyes
flickered open, and Tom was
relieved to see that the fire was
back, swirling in their depths. Epos
pushed herself up with her wings
and got to her feet, shaking her
ruffled feathers. Tom put his hand
to his red jewel. *I wish you a good
flight, friend!* he told the Beast.

Epos extended her wings, and Tom
and Elenna lifted their hands in
farewell as she rose into the sky. Tom
watched as Epos soared towards
the pale winter sun hanging low
over the eastern horizon. Then a
tremendous shiver of cold grabbed
hold of him, and he quickly pulled
his cloak back on.

"Are you okay?" Elenna asked.

Tom nodded. "Let's go and find Nanook."

Tom and Elenna trudged across the snowy ground as quickly as they could. But with each footstep, they plunged through a crust of freezing powder and sank up their knees. It was hard going, and soon Tom's lungs burned with cold and tiredness. His whole body was covered in a layer of freezing sweat. Tom scanned the flat, white landscape all around them, looking for any sign of Nanook. The bright snow was painful to look at, and he had to keep rubbing his eyes and blinking away tears.

Suddenly Elenna gasped. "Tom, look!" she said, pointing. Tom could

see a line of deep craters in the snow
– huge footsteps, and around them,
scarlet patches of frozen blood. Tom
followed the line of the footsteps
with his eyes, using the magic of his
golden helmet to enhance his sight.
His chest tightened with horror at
what he saw. Ahead, Nanook's huge,

shaggy form lay slumped in the snow.
The ice around her was churned up,
as if there had been a tremendous
struggle, and there were more bright
red spatters of blood. As Tom and
Elenna pounded towards her, Elenna
cried out in dismay. "Nanook! What's
happened to her?"

Tom could see that one of the Beast's front paws was clutched to her chest, partly covering a gaping wound. Her face was scrunched up in pain. Suddenly, her blue eyes flickered open. At the sight of Tom and Elenna pounding towards her, they went wide with fear.

Stay back... Tom heard Nanook's voice echoing in his mind. *Beware the Ice Marauders!*

Tom heard a harsh cry from behind him, almost like the sound of splintering ice. He and Elenna spun around to see a pack of hunched, goblin-like creatures, made entirely of ice. Tom stared at their strange attackers, an uneasy fear creeping over him. The creatures were like

nothing he'd encountered before.
Their eyes glowed with the bright,
deadly blue of new meltwater, and in
their hands they held sturdy axes and
long, curved knives which glittered
coldly in the sun.

MENACE IN THE NORTH

Tom lifted his blade, ready for the attack, and Elenna snatched her bow from her back and quickly took aim.

"Craaaaarrr," rasped one of the ice goblins, bigger than the rest, swinging his arm towards Tom and Elenna. At their leader's signal, the creatures lumbered forwards, skirting over the top of the deep snow and reaching the

more tightly packed ground around
Tom and Elenna. Their blue eyes
glinted hungrily as they waved their
shining weapons. Tom lunged as the
first came into range. The ice goblin
sent its axe crashing downwards
towards Tom's head, but Tom blocked
the blow with his shield, then swiped
upwards with his sword. He heard
a splintering crack as his blade
smashed through the creature's arm,
and the severed limb fell, shattering
into glittering shards. The goblin's
mouth gaped. Tom watched in
horrified amazement as the wounded
monster tugged a knife from its belt
with its remaining hand, and lurched
on as if it had not felt a thing.

Elenna's arrow whistled past Tom,

hitting the ice goblin in the chest. The
creature exploded into tiny fragments
which glanced through the air and
pattered against Tom's cloak. He felt
a sharp pain as one shard slashed his
cheek.

Another creature was already
lunging towards him, wielding a

pale, glistening knife. Two more surged forwards to join it. Tom flicked out his sword, swiping the first aside; then he slashed left and right across the other creatures' chests, smashing them to pieces. His pulse was beating fast now, and he was starting to feel warm under his cloak. There were at least twenty more of the monsters, but Tom was ready for them. He hunkered down low and lifted his blade before him as they eyed him from a distance, muttering in harsh, sharp voices. Another of Elenna's arrows hummed through the freezing air.

Smash! The creature at the centre of the group splintered into a shimmering cloud of ice crystals.

The others let out piercing screeches of rage, then turned and fled, their long arms swinging by their sides. As they loped away, Tom saw the largest of the creatures glance back at him. Its blue gaze burned with a mindless rage that filled Tom's belly with a gnawing dread.

He turned to Elenna. She was squinting after the ice goblins along the shaft of an arrow, but finally she lowered her bow. "It looks like we've frightened them off," she said.

Tom nodded. "But we'll have to be wary. I've a feeling they'll be back for more. I've never even heard of such creatures."

"We used to tell tales of Ice Marauders in the winter," Elenna said. "Back when I was small. Vicious demons made of ice that feel no pain and have no mercy. But I never thought they were real!" She shivered, wrapping her cloak tighter around herself.

Tom shrugged. "This is Avantia," he said. "By now, we should be used to the fact that anything's possible."

Elenna sighed. "True," she said, "but why can't it be Mother Midwinter, with her baskets of cakes and biscuits, that turns out to be true, instead of those cowardly pack hunters?"

Tom and Elenna trudged across the snow to where the wounded Good Beast lay curled up, her eyes closed and her arms clutched across her chest. Tom put his hand on her side, and called on the power of his red jewel.

"Nanook?" he said, as Elenna gently stroked the Beast's fur. "Are you awake?" Nanook let out a throaty growl and her eyes flickered open. She frowned at Tom, as if trying to see him clearly.

Nanook's voice spoke in his mind. *I am hurt*, she said. *I need to rest, but the marauders bite and claw at me. I am so tired!*

Tom took Epos's talon from his shield, and held it against the bloody gash in Nanook's chest. The Beast flinched, but didn't pull away. Tom concentrated on the cut, focussing the healing powers of Epos's talon.

As he moved the magical token along the length of the wound, the edges knitted together. Tom ran his fingers through Nanook's fur, finding more cuts and grazes, and healing each as he went. Finally, he turned his attention to Nanook's leg, bent at an unnatural angle below the knee. He removed the green jewel from his belt and held it against the broken bone. With a gentle clicking sound, the bone shifted back into place, and Tom heard Nanook let out a long, rumbling growl of relief.

The shaggy giant pulled herself up onto all fours and shook her pelt. Then she gave an angry grunt and stood straight and as tall as a tree. Tom smiled at the sight of her well again, although she still seemed a little shaky as she lifted her face to the sky and sniffed, then turned towards him.

Too much snow, Nanook told Tom, moving her massive arms in a wide arc. Her voice in his mind sounded angry, but Tom sensed fear as well. *Too much ice*, she said. *Darkness rises in the North. Yakorix wakes. I started south to warn the king, but Yakorix found me. We fought a mighty battle, but Yakorix is strong.*

The Beast raised one big, leathery paw and placed it on Tom's chest with a gentleness that surprised him. *Thank you*, she said.

Tom touched the red jewel in his belt. "Nanook?" Tom asked the Beast.

"Do you think you can take us to
this new danger in the North?"

Nanook lifted her head and sniffed
again, then scanned the white,
windswept plain about them. She
nodded. Then she turned her face
into the wind, and started off across

the snow and ice.

Tom and Elenna followed. As they trudged across the icy plain, the sun swept in a long, slow arc across the horizon, casting shimmering pink patterns onto the wispy clouds. The wind whistled over the land, throwing up eddies of glittering snow and tugging at Tom's cloak. Where the wind pierced the protection of the magical garment, the chill sliced right to the bone. Tom glanced at Elenna, and saw that her teeth were gritted against the cold.

At that moment, the wind gave a sudden, screeching howl and whirled around them. The sunlight seemed to waver, then vanish, and when Tom looked to the sky, he saw piles of towering dark clouds sweeping towards them. The snow hit all at once – small, sharp flakes, like scouring sand.

"Elenna! Get behind me, quick!" Tom shouted, holding his shield up before him to use Nanook's bell to protect them from the cold gusts.

Nanook turned her nose to the air and drew another short breath, her pale form almost hidden by the driving snow. *An Evil storm*, she told Tom. Then she turned and trudged on through the blizzard, her broad shoulders hunched and her shaggy fur pulled straight behind her by the fierce gale.

Tom followed, keeping his shield held high. He focussed on Nanook's back, the only solid thing in the whirling whiteness. His eyes stung from the gritty, driving snow. His legs and arms felt stiff and heavy and every footstep jolted through him with raw pain from his half-frozen feet.

Then, as abruptly as it started, the snow stopped and the buffeting gale died. Tom almost toppled forwards. He blinked in the sudden glare of the sun, then shook his head, unable to believe what he was seeing.

A huge, snow-covered mountain loomed before them, with a flat, pitted top. Built into the side was a palace made of ice. Needle-sharp spires pointed skywards and glittering windows shone in

the weak winter sun.

Beside Tom, Elenna let out a long
breath. "It's beautiful!" she said.

Nanook grunted, and Tom put
his hand to his red jewel. He heard
Nanook's warning: *Danger lies
within that place.*

The Good Beast started off
again towards the ice palace. As
Tom got closer, he could see that a
high, translucent wall of blue ice
surrounded the structure. Before
the wall, the land fell away into
a wide chasm, like the jagged rift
created by a mighty earthquake.
A broad bridge of ice spanned the
chasm, leading to a passage through
the wall.

Something moved at the edge of
Tom's vision. Nanook howled in
warning and Tom's hand rushed to
his sword hilt as he squinted ahead,
his pulse quickening.

"What is it?" cried Elenna.

A vast shape stepped from the
deep blue shadow of the passageway

and out onto the bridge of ice.
Tom's grip tightened and his heart
thumped harder. It was like a bear,
and as white as the snow, but with
a row of dark, tooth-like spikes
along its back. The Beast radiated
power and hatred. It was taller even
than Nanook, and its eyes glowed a
putrid yellow, like poisoned flames.
Tom could see that its cruel claws
ended in sharp points, and when it
parted its lips in a snarl, it bared
curved yellow teeth, each as long as
Tom's arm.

Tom stared at the Beast – an
ancient creature arisen from legend.
"Yakorix!"

As if in answer, the ice bear
dropped to all fours and barrelled

towards them with the deadly speed
and power of an avalanche.

5

A MIGHTY BATTLE

The ice bridge juddered beneath the Beast's paws. Tom lifted his sword, still holding his shield high to protect himself and Elenna from the cold. Nanook bared her teeth and raised her fists before her face, and Elenna scrabbled for her bow.

As Yakorix leapt from the bridge and raced across the icy plain, Tom dropped into a low, fighting stance.

The Beast charged onwards like a raging bull, great clouds of glittering ice churning up behind her. Tom's whole body shook with the rumbling of the earth. Soon he could see every detail of the Beast's bear-like face. Her lips were pulled back in a hideous snarl, and her yellow eyes blazed as she ducked her head and cannoned towards them. *She's going to run us down!* Tom realised.

"Move!" he shouted. Nanook leapt sideways. Tom and Elenna threw themselves the other way, but Yakorix turned in mid-stride and reared, swiping at Nanook with her pointed claws. The Good Beast bellowed and fell to the ground, her scarlet blood spattering the snow as the Ice Bear spun. The spines on Yakorix's back glinted as her front paws came down with an earth-shaking thud, and her back legs kicked out. The Beast's giant, shaggy paws flew towards Tom and Elenna like the hooves of a furious horse. Tom shifted his shield to catch the blow and Elenna leapt behind him.

SMASH! The shield flew from Tom's grip and he shot backwards, slamming into Elenna with so much power they both fell and skidded across the ice. As Tom slid to a stop, the cold hit him with a force even greater than Yakorix's kick. Beside him, Elenna cried out and rolled into a ball. Without Nanook's bell, Daltec's magic cloaks were too weak

to protect them from the enchanted
cold this far north. Tom looked
desperately for his shield and spotted
it half buried in the snow a few
footsteps away. He leapt to his feet
and snatched it up. Elenna scrambled
behind the shield, and Tom's body

shuddered with relief to be out of the deadly cold.

A tremendous bellow of rage echoed around them, vibrating the air in Tom's chest. He looked up to see Yakorix standing high on her hind legs, swiping at Nanook. The Good Beast was snarling and blocking with her fists, trying to fend off the blows, but she was still weak from Yakorix's first ambush, and the attacks of the Ice Marauders. As Tom watched, Yakorix grabbed Nanook by the shoulders and dug her claws in deep. Nanook let out a roar that shook the mountain. She struggled in the Beast's grip, but Yakorix held her fast.

"Stay behind me!" Tom told Elenna, then lifted his sword, and

charged towards Yakorix. The two
arctic Beasts were grappling now,
each trying to force the other down.
Yakorix threw her massive weight
against Nanook's chest. The force
bent the Snow Monster backwards.
She growled in pain, her blue eyes
flashing with anger and her sharp

claws swiping at Yakorix's thick arms.
Tom's blood beat hot in his veins as he
raced to join the fight. But before he
could reach his friend, Yakorix turned.
Her glowing yellow eyes locked with
Tom's. She lifted her mighty hind paw
and stamped.

BOOM! A ripple ran through the
frozen ground. Tom stumbled and fell.
Elenna came down hard beside him. As
they scrambled to their feet, Tom saw
Yakorix lift Nanook in her powerful
arms, then dash her to the ground.
Nanook rolled, and lay panting on her
back. Yakorix pounced and landed
astride Nanook, pinning her.

Tom rushed forward desperately,
Elenna right behind. He stared in
horror as the giant bear Beast swiped

again and again at Nanook's face.
Nanook batted the blows aside with
her powerful paws. But Tom could
see that the Good Beast was tiring.
Yakorix's terrible claws raked across
her fur, sending an arc of blood over
the ice. Tom felt torn. *To help Nanook,
I'll need to use my magical tokens,
but that would mean leaving Elenna
behind. And without the warmth
from Nanook's bell, she will freeze to
death.*

"Go!" Elenna cried. "Help her. I'll be
all right!"

Tom nodded, grateful for his
friend's bravery. Then he called on
the power of his golden leg armour
and launched himself forwards.
Anger and fear for Nanook surged

through him as his feet sped over the ground, skirting the top of the snow. As he drew close, he bent his knees and leapt towards Yakorix, landing a powerful two-legged kick to the side of her head.

Yakorix let out a roar as she was

thrown from Nanook's chest. She landed on her belly with a crash then skidded, her sharp paws scrabbling at the ice. Just before Yakorix reached the chasm-like moat that ran around the frozen palace, she dug her claws into the ice, and came to a stop.

Nanook leapt up and let out a bellow of rage. She hurtled forwards and threw herself onto the Ice Bear, raining blow after blow down onto the Evil Beast.

Tom lifted his sword, casting a worried glance back to Elenna who was huddled in the snow.

"Go!" she cried, lifting one arm beneath her robe and pointing towards Yakorix.

Tom was about to race in to drive

their advantage home, but at that moment Yakorix forced herself to her feet, slamming her full weight against Nanook. Nanook staggered backwards, bellowing in pain, her huge paw impaled on the dark spikes that ran down their enemy's back. Yakorix let out a mighty snarl of rage then threw herself forwards onto all fours, yanking Nanook from her feet by the paw and sending her whirling through the air. The Good Beast disappeared over the lip of the chasm. Tom's heart gave a painful leap as he saw his friend vanish from sight. A terrible thud echoed around him, sickening him to the core.

FIGHTING THE ICE BEAR

Nanook! Tom feared the Snow Monster had been injured by her fall. *I just hope she's still alive.*

Yakorix lifted her muzzle high into the air and let out a triumphant roar, beating her chest. Tom drew a deep breath of freezing air and squared his shoulders. *I am the Master of the Beasts*, he told himself. *That brute will pay for her treatment of Nanook!* He called on the power of his golden leg armour and raced towards Yakorix. The great bear turned towards him, her yellow eyes flashing with the hungry light of a hunter scenting prey. Tom lifted his sword. He summoned the power of his golden gauntlets and felt his mind grow sharp, his hands sure and steady on the hilt.

His blade sang as he sent it swishing downwards towards Yakorix's chest. The Beast threw up her paws to deflect the blow but Tom's sword sliced past them with the enhanced skill and speed from his gauntlets. Silvery light glistened along its length as he brought it down

again and again, slicing at the Beast's thick pelt and broad, powerful arms.

Yakorix roared and flailed at him, trying to claw at his face, but Tom spun and lunged, fury powering through his veins. The tip of his blade flickered through the air, slashing at the Beast's white fur and leaving dark red welts. Yakorix leapt back, her hot breath rising on the freezing air and her eyes narrowed with rage. She lowered her head, and cannoned towards him. Tom sprang to one side, swinging his blade in a wide arc across her back as she approached, slicing the tips from the dark spikes that ran along her spine.

Yakorix roared in pain, her body shuddering and her head thrashing from side to side. She turned and stomped away, leaving a trail of red droplets in the snow as she raced back across the bridge to the ice palace. As soon as she reached the shadow of the ice wall, she swiped at a lever with her paw. The bridge of ice

started to rise. Tom called on
the power of his golden boots and
bent his knees, ready to leap the
chasm after the Beast, but a thin
and desperate cry reached him on the
icy wind.

"Tom!" Elenna's voice sounded so
weak. Tom spun and darted towards
his friend, who was huddled on the
ice with her knees drawn up to her
chest and her cloak wrapped tightly
about her. Her skin was as white as
the snow, and her lashes and fringe
were coated with frost.

"I'm s-s-s-s-so c-c-c-cold," Elenna
shivered. Tom lifted his shield over
his friend so the power of Nanook's
magical bell could warm her. Elenna's
shivering quickly slowed. "We must

help Nanook!" she said.

As if in answer, Tom heard a bellow of rage echo from the chasm surrounding the ice palace. The knot of dread in his stomach loosened at the sound. *She's alive!*

Elenna struggled to her feet. Tom held his shield before them both as they raced over the ice towards the chasm where Nanook had fallen. He looked over the edge to see the Good Beast pacing backwards and forwards far below, her blue eyes burning bright with fury. The sides of the chasm were sheer, and covered in a crust of slippery ice. There were no hand or footholds at all.

"Don't worry," Tom told the furious Beast. "We'll find a way to get you out.

But first, we need to stop Yakorix."
Tom turned to Elenna. "We have to
get into the palace."

Elenna ran her eyes over the smooth
chasm walls and frowned. "Let's
follow the moat around," she said.
"Maybe it leads to another bridge."

Tom nodded, and started to follow
the edge of the rift, but Nanook let
out a sharp warning cry. Something
whistled through the air and thudded
into the snow before Tom's feet. It was
an arrow made of ice.

"Tom, look!" Elenna cried, pointing
up into the battlements of the castle.
A row of grinning Ice Marauders
leered back at them, each with a bow
and arrow of glittering ice aimed
straight at Tom and Elenna.

EVIL IN THE WIND

"Duck!" Tom told Elenna, throwing his shield up against the hail of needle-sharp arrows pelting towards them. He felt a painful jolt in his arm as each arrow crashed into his shield and shattered into a shower of icy shards. He could hear thin, hollow howls like the screech of the wind, and the crack of icy laughter from the creatures above. More arrows clattered against his shield, and Tom's muscles started to ache from the strain of withstanding the barrage.

"If you shelter me with the shield," Elenna said, "I can return fire from behind you."

"I'll do my best," Tom said. He knelt down, called on the power of his golden breastplate to give him superhuman strength, then braced himself against the next onslaught of missiles. Elenna pulled her bow from her back, and strung an arrow. Her fingers were chapped and red with the cold, but her hands were steady. Tom glanced over the top of his shield as she let her arrow fly. It soared over the battlements of the ice palace and struck a marauder in the chest.

The monster exploded in a spray of glittering ice. Elenna took aim again.

Crash! Another marauder fell to pieces. Tom could see the creatures turning to look at each other with frowns of dismay. Another of Elenna's arrows struck, and the monsters let out howls of rage – but, for every creature that Elenna destroyed, two more took its place. For each arrow that she fired, an answering hail of arrows thudded against Tom's shield.

"It's no good!" Elenna said at last. "There are just too many of them!"

"We need another plan," Tom said. "Let's head around the mountain. Maybe we can climb it and approach the castle from behind where it won't be so well guarded."

"That would be an excellent plan," Elenna said, "if we weren't likely to get skewered by an ice arrow on the way."

"I've thought of that," Tom said. "I'll use the power of my leg armour to dodge between the shafts. You can ride on my back."

Elenna frowned, but then she nodded. "I suppose I don't have much choice," she said.

Tom waited while Elenna hopped onto his back and hooked her arms around his neck, then he leapt to his feet and ran. *Whoa!* An arrow zoomed straight for Tom's face, but he sidestepped it.

Two more arrows seared towards his legs and he jumped into the air, skidding back to the ice. He raced as fast as his leg armour would carry him, dodging left and right between the falling arrows. With the magical strength from his golden breastplate, Elenna felt very light, and soon they were rounding the mountain, out of range of the marauders' fire.

Tom set Elenna down, and turned to look at the view. The mountain towered high above them. It was covered in snow, and glittering icicles hung from every outcrop. Before their feet, the deep chasm curved around the huge mountain, and the sides were steep and smooth. Tom shook his head in dismay. He couldn't see any way to cross.

"How nice of you to pay me a visit,"

a low female voice echoed from above
them. Tom looked up to see a tall,
slender figure standing in the mouth
of a cave high on the mountain's side.
Icicles hung all around her, and she
was dressed in a shining green gown.
Her hair whipped about her head,

framing her pale face like a halo of licking flames. Her scarlet lips were spread into an evil grin.

Kensa! Tom felt a terrible rage building inside him as the witch raised her lightning staff.

"It is the last visit you will ever make!" Kensa cried, her green eyes shining with a poisonous light. "This time, I will not fail in my mission. The endless winter has arrived and it will bring Avantia to its knees!"

STORY TWO

For centuries, Avantia has been ruled from the City, but the age of ice is upon us now. Soon King Hugo's palace will be buried under snow and I will rule from my mountain fortress. I will watch from my battlements as the land and its people freeze.

So the young warriors have made it past my Ice Marauders. No matter! They are living on borrowed time. The only question is whether they will die at the claws of Yakorix or if the cold will turn the blood to ice in their veins first.

The thought of their deaths warms me better than any fire.

Come to me, "heroes" of Avantia. Come to your doom!

Kensa, Queen of the Frozen Kingdom

DARK FORCES

Kensa raised her lighting staff
skywards, her face lit up with
cruel joy.

"Avantia will be mine!" she cried.

Tom shook his head, the anger
inside him hardening to fierce
determination. *Not while there's
blood in my veins!* he vowed. He
glared back at the witch. "I should
have guessed you'd be at the heart of

this unnatural winter!" he cried. "But if you think you can destroy Avantia, you're living in a fairy tale!"

Kensa tipped her head back, and gave a long, throaty chuckle. "Am I indeed?" she said. "I brought Yakorix back from the legends, and now I plan to unleash powers more terrifying than even your darkest fireside tales."

Kensa's final words snapped like the lash of a whip, and Tom suddenly realised exactly where he stood. *This is the volcano from the stories! The one Yakorix fell into all those many years ago!* He felt the hairs on the back of his neck stirring as Kensa started to chant in a high-pitched voice. Her words rose on the freezing wind, loud and harsh, but in a strange language Tom did not know. *What evil spell is she casting now?*

As Tom watched, the wind started to swirl around the witch, drawing dark clouds ever closer towards her through the sky.

"We have to stop her!" Elenna cried, shouting to be heard over the rising wind. She lifted her bow and let an arrow fly, but it was snatched up by the growing storm and dashed against the volcano's side. Kensa's eyes had rolled back in her head, her chanting rising to a wild cry. Clouds swooped and whirled above her. Tom could feel the strength of the evil wind tugging at his shield, almost lifting him from his feet. He dug in his heels and braced himself, using all of his strength to keep his shield from being snatched from his grasp.

Suddenly a fork of lighting crackled down, striking the tip of Kensa's staff. Ice crystals burst outwards in a flash of dazzling blue light. They swirled in the wind that raged around the enchantress until she stood at the centre of a vortex surrounded by glittering flying shards. Kensa turned her staff and thrust the tip towards Tom and Elenna, her red lips curled into a vicious grin. Then she stepped back and vanished into the shadows of her cave.

Tom felt a shock of fear as thousands of deadly ice daggers swooped down from the mountain straight towards him. He leapt in front of Elenna and threw up his shield up to protect them both from the jagged spikes of ice, but the spinning column whirled straight past them.

Tom turned to see the spiral of ice split into swirling eddies. He felt a terrible blast of cold, so fierce it

burned the skin of his hands and face. Elenna gasped in pain.

As the first of the enchanted whirlwinds touched the ground, the ice crystals drew together into a slender shape with piercing pale-blue eyes. *An Ice Marauder!*

"Tom, watch out!" Elenna cried, as the evil creature sprang towards him and swung a hefty two-headed axe. Tom lifted his sword and sent it crashing down, straight though the creature's wrist. The axe went skittering across the ice, still clutched in the marauder's frozen fingers. The creature gave an angry rasp and leapt after its severed hand. But more marauders were already forming, drawing together from the spinning twisters of sleety snow.

A pair of the monsters stepped forward together, baring their pointed teeth as they lifted long, curved knives. Elenna darted past Tom and leapt, landing a hefty kick to one of the monsters' chests. It toppled backwards and shattered as Tom lunged and smacked the other over the head with the flat of his sword. The monster's head exploded, but to Tom's horrified surprise, the headless creature lurched onwards, swinging its axe for his chest. Tom lifted his sword...

Clang! The weapons met with a shock that rang painfully along Tom's arm. His sword was wrenched from his fingers and the ice monster staggered on. Tom swung his fist for the creature's chest, but before his blow connected, the monster's long arms whipped forwards. Icy fingers clutched Tom's neck and squeezed. The pain was instant – piercing cold seared Tom's skin and shot down his neck to his chest, like a freezing knife to the heart. He gasped as all the muscles in his body locked tight – he was unable to move, or even breathe!

"Tom!" Elenna raced to his side and tried to prise away the fingers that gripped his neck, gasping with pain when she touched the icy flesh.

"Let go of him!" Elenna cried, lifting her bow like a club, but another Ice Marauder let out a brittle laugh and launched itself towards

her. Elenna kicked out, sending the marauder flying, but another was already rushing forwards to take its place.

Tom jolted into action, forcing his mind to ignore the terrible burning pain at his neck and ordering his muscles to unlock. He called on the strength of his magical breastplate and brought his arms upwards and outwards, breaking the marauder's grip on his throat. As the creature staggered back, Tom grabbed hold of it, lifting it up and hurling it with all his magical strength.

SMASH! The headless monster collided with the rest of the goblin-like creatures, who tumbled over like skittles, shattering as they fell. Transparent limbs and body parts skittered out across the ice in all directions. But the fallen marauders didn't stay down. Tom felt his terror building as the headless and armless monsters started scrambling to their feet. And more were still appearing from the whirling winds behind them.

"There are too many to fight," shouted Elenna.

Tom turned to his friend, whose eyes were wide with horror. "Run!" he said. They both turned and raced towards the moat. "We have to get across!" Tom cried, staring at the deep shadowy crevasse. *But how?*

INSIDE THE ICE PALACE

Tom's mind raced as he pounded towards the deep chasm. There was only one way both he and Elenna could get across. It was risky, but they'd have to try it or Kensa's Ice Marauders would cut them to pieces.

Tom called on the speed from his magic leg armour, and the strength of his breastplate. He felt the power flowing into his freezing muscles, returning their strength and vigour. Tom called over his shoulder to Elenna, "When I say 'now', jump onto my back." Elenna nodded. They raced on, almost to the brink. As the chasm curved away before them, Tom put all his focus into harnessing every bit of power from his Golden Armour.

"Now!" he cried. Just as Elenna landed on his back and wrapped her arms around his neck, Tom bent his knees and leapt. Icy air whistled past and the ground plunged away below him. He heard Elenna gasp as they soared over the chasm.

Thud! Tom landed on the far side of the moat, his heart lurching with terror as he felt the edge start to

crumble under his boot. He threw
himself forwards, away from the gap,
landing hard on his stomach. Elenna
flew off and hit the ground in a roll.
They both quickly scrambled up, and
glanced back to see the ice monsters
waving their axes and howling on the
far side of the crevasse.

"Quick!" Tom said, gesturing for Elenna to follow him into the shadow of the ice wall that surrounded the volcano, keeping low to avoid being spotted by the ice guards. Eventually, they reached the high drawbridge that Tom had seen Yakorix open. It was made from a huge block of ice, carved all over with the shapes of bears and wolves. Deep in a fissure beside the door, Tom could see a curved handle shaped like a claw.

He turned to Elenna. "Be ready for an attack," he said. "Yakorix may be waiting on the other side." Elenna hunched down beside the door and took aim with her bow.

Tom tried the handle. It turned easily, and the huge ice drawbridge started to lower smoothly and silently over the chasm. Tom peered through the doorway to see a broad courtyard beyond. There was no sign of Yakorix. Elenna lowered her bow and got up.

Together, they stepped inside the thick, blue wall of ice. Tom could feel a stinging cold coming from the shimmering surface. As they entered the courtyard, Elenna gasped in awe. The open space was filled with jagged crystals of ice. Every surface shone pink and gold and turquoise, reflecting the wintry sky. Massive steps of ice rose up at the back of the courtyard, climbing the side of the volcano towards the palace.

The palace itself glittered like the blade of a knife. It had slender, pointed towers like cruel teeth and a tall entrance in the shape of a dagger.

Tom kept his shield raised against the bitter cold as they crossed the courtyard and climbed the steps towards the entrance. Tom glanced warily about them as they went, but nothing stirred in the expanse of ice except the biting wind.

"We need to find Kensa," he said. Their footsteps rang on the ground as they stepped through the open doorway to find themselves in a huge, shady chamber of thick blue ice.

Elenna shuddered. "If anything, it's colder in here than outside!" she said. Her voice echoed off translucent pillars of ice that reached to the domed ceiling above.

Tom and Elenna's breath rose in cloudy puffs, and Tom could feel the soles of his boots creaking on the icy ground. He led Elenna towards another pointed arch at the far end of the room. A long corridor stretched away before them, lit by glowing blue ice spheres set into niches in the wall.

As they followed the shadowy corridor, the only sounds Tom could hear were the crunch of their boots on ice and the rasp of air in their freezing lungs. The passageway led them deeper and deeper into the mountain, until Tom's arms ached from holding up his shield.

"Where do you think Kensa is?" Elenna whispered.

"She has to be in here somewhere,"

Tom said. "We need to find her and
undo whatever she's done to create
this terrible winter." Tom fell silent.
He could feel a faint tremor in the
ground. He put a finger to his lips and
listened hard. A deep rumble echoed
down the corridor towards him.

"Yakorix's footsteps!" Tom said.

"She must be somewhere nearby."

Elenna shook her head. "That doesn't sound like footsteps to me," she said, turning to glance behind her. "It sounds more like... Watch out!"

Tom turned to see a huge boulder of ice tumbling towards them.

ELENNA'S SACRIFICE

"Run!" Tom shouted as he turned and sprinted away across the slippery ground, heading deeper into the heart of the mountain. He could hear Elenna's footsteps close behind him and the rumble of the ice boulder gaining on them, fast. Soon the sound was all around them, like the echo of thunder in the mountains. Tom thought of using his magical leg armour, but the extra speed on the treacherous ground was risky, and if they slipped...

Tom glanced back, and his heart leapt into his throat at the sight of the giant sphere of crushing ice right at Elenna's heels. He scanned the

corridor as he ran, looking for any way to escape – but it seemed to go on forever. There was a shallow alcove to the right, holding a glowing sphere. It looked barely big enough to hold Elenna, let alone both of them, but it would have to do. "In there!" Tom cried, skidding to a stop as Elenna ducked into the alcove. Tom bundled in behind her, throwing himself in front of his friend, and holding his shield up to cover the entrance. He sucked in his breath and shrank back against Elenna as the ice boulder thundered past.

BOOM! Tom felt a shock run along his arms as the ball of ice smashed into his shield, tearing it from his fingers. "My shield!" Tom shouted as it was carried away on the rolling white mound. The boulder tumbled on down the corridor, leaving Tom's shield pressed into the ice about fifty paces away. Tom's teeth chattered uncontrollably. *We need the warmth of Nanook's bell to survive!* But his muscles were locked, and his body racked with painful shivering. Fifty paces might as well be the other side of the kingdom.

"I-I-I h-have to t-t-try," he said, his teeth chattering so hard he couldn't get out the rest of the words.

"Take this," Elenna said, thrusting her cloak towards him. "Qu-qu-quick!"

Tom knew it was the only way. He threw Elenna's cloak over his own, and felt the terrible cold recede – not much, but enough for his stiff limbs to unlock. He stumbled forwards. His feet were like clumsy lumps of wood, and he could hardly feel his fingers, but he pushed himself onwards until the shield was almost within reach. *I need to get the shield back to Elenna before she perishes.* His whole body ached for the warmth of Nanook's bell. *Just a few more steps...*

"Not so fast!" a cruel voice boomed behind him. Tom turned to see Kensa pacing towards him. Her long green gown swept along the floor behind her, and her stride was quick and easy. She didn't seem to feel the cold at all. Then Tom noticed she was wearing a glowing pendant around

her neck which pulsed with amber
light.

A magical talisman, he realised. *It
must be keeping her warm.*

Kensa passed the alcove where
Elenna's shivering body lay huddled
without so much as a glance, then

strode onwards towards Tom. She stopped, and her lips spread into an evil grin. Tom gritted his teeth to control his shivering and rage.

"I've been waiting for this chance for a long time," Kensa said, her hair glinting in the silvery light. "This is the moment I see you die!" She lifted her staff, and darted forwards, swinging the crystal tip towards Tom's face.

AN ICY TOMB

The crystal tip of Kensa's staff
flashed through the air. Tom forced
his stiff arms to move, calling on
the power of his golden gauntlets
as he used his sword to bat the staff
clumsily aside. But the shock of the
impact left his frozen hand stinging.
Her green eyes glinting, Kensa
jabbed her staff towards his chest.

Tom swiped his sword upwards,

but it was like trying to move
through treacle. His arms moved so
slowly!

Kensa's staff swished towards
him again. *Smack!* The pain jolted
through Tom's frozen body and he
lost his balance, toppling backwards
onto the ice. The shock of the fall

was almost too much. Everything hurt and none of his limbs seemed to work.

For a moment Tom just lay, unable to summon the strength to stand. Suddenly Kensa let out a yelp of pain and Tom looked up to see Elenna wielding her bow like a club and the witch clutching the back of her head. But then Kensa spun, and sent her staff swishing round, right into Elenna's chest. Elenna was slammed against the tunnel wall and fell to the ground, gasping for breath. She lay slumped where she fell, her whole body shuddering with cold, her face white. Kensa scowled and sent the sharp toe of her boot hard into Elenna's stomach.

At the sight of his friend bent double, fury powered through Tom's veins, warming his icy blood. He scrambled to his feet and dived forwards, swinging his sword as he lunged. But at the sound of his feet on the ice, Kensa spun, her staff swiping through the air. Tom leapt sideways, but Kensa pounced, and her staff stabbed towards him again. Tom swung his sword, but he was shivering so hard he couldn't keep the blade steady. Kensa batted it aside and lashed her staff towards his face.

Crack! Tom fell backwards and skidded across the ice towards Elenna as a sharp pain blossomed in his cheek. The two of them lay gasping for breath, their bodies curled to protect them from the enchanted cold.

"Not so brave now, eh?" Kensa said. "I knew it! You're nothing more than a village boy with a bunch of trinkets and amulets."

Tom could feel his anger building again. *Kensa won't beat me!* he told himself. He swallowed his rage, letting it burn in the pit of his stomach. Then he sprang to his feet, calling on the magic of his leg armour to race towards the witch. Kensa threw her staff up to shield herself, but Tom wasn't thinking of swordplay any more. He leapt forwards and landed in a skid, cannoning into his enemy's legs.

"Aargh!" Kensa was knocked from her feet, her eyes wide and her arms flailing. Tom didn't look back to see how she landed. He slid onwards until he reached his shield, then he snatched it up. The warmth of Nanook's bell thawed his aching muscles, like a hot, steamy bath. Tom let out a long sigh as the pain and the stiffness left his body. Then he spun around to face Kensa. She had managed to get to her feet and was backing away from him down the corridor.

"Where are you going?" Tom shouted after her. "Are you too afraid to fight me now that I'm no longer close to death?"

The witch laughed. "I don't have to fight you, child," she said. Tom felt the ground start to quake with the steady rhythm of mighty footsteps. It was a sound that filled him with dread.

Yakorix.

Kensa grinned. "You will never

escape this palace," she said. "The bones of you and your little friend will lie buried under ice while Avantia freezes forever!" She let out a wild laugh, then turned and ran. Elenna made a grab for Kensa's legs as the Evil Witch raced by, but her movements were slow and clumsy. She missed, her arms swiping at the frozen air as Kensa streaked away.

Tom's heart jolted as he saw Elenna's head sink down onto the ice. Her eyes were half shut, and her skin was as pale as wax. *Without her cloak, she'll freeze to death!*

Tom raced towards his friend to protect her with his shield, but something snagged his cloak from behind. He felt a hot breath on the

back of his neck, and the sudden
agony of sharp claws digging into
his shoulder blade. Tom let out a cry,
paralysed by pain.

The Beast had caught him.

5

BATTLE IN THE THRONE ROOM

Tom tried to twist himself free of
Yakorix's grip but felt himself lifted
into the air like a rag doll, the Beast's
claws piercing his shoulder. Tom tried
to turn, but the huge Beast tossed
him over her shoulder. The wind
was knocked from Tom's lungs and
pain seared through his chest. His
body juddered as Yakorix turned and

pounded away, with Tom slung across her back.

Tom heard a gasp ahead of him and pressed his fists into the bear's back, raising his head. "Elenna!" His friend was still curled on the floor, reaching

a pale hand helplessly towards him. Tom reached a hand up to his neck and hurriedly tugged at the fastening of Elenna's cloak. *If I don't get this off, she'll freeze.* Eventually, the cloak came loose and Tom pulled it from his body, letting it fall to the ground, just as Yakorix turned a corner. Tom lost sight of his friend's anguished face. *She'll reach the cloak*, he told himself. *She has to!*

Every step that Yakorix took sent a stab of pain through Tom's wounded shoulder. He clung tight to his shield as he was joggled up and down in the grip of the mighty Beast. *Nanook's bell is the only thing that will give me enough warmth to be able to fight back.*

Finally, the tunnel came to an end and Tom was carried into a vast, circular chamber. He pushed the pain from his mind, preparing for the battle to come. Without warning, Yakorix hefted him from her back, swung him by the arms and sent him spinning through the air. Shimmering ice whizzed by Tom's face and his stomach lurched. His spinning vision picked out a carved throne of ice...

Crash! Tom's body slammed against the throne, smashing it to pieces. Pain racked his body. Somehow he'd managed to keep hold of his shield and he clutched it to his chest as he lay winded and bruised amid the ruins of the icy chair. He was facing upwards, with the vaulted ceiling arching away far above him. High on the wall, around the edge of the circular room, ran a narrow balcony carved from ice. Looming over him from the raised platform, a triumphant grin spread across her evil face, stood Kensa.

Tom shook his head to clear his thoughts. *I have to fight*, he told himself, ignoring his pain and the cold. *For Elenna and for all of Avantia.*

He pushed himself slowly to his feet. Yakorix was waiting for him in the centre of the room, her huge paws raised before her and her long teeth dripping with drool. She lifted her muzzle and let out a low, rumbling snarl.

Tom's sword had never felt so heavy, as the cold made even the strength of his Golden Armour seep away. He could barely feel the hilt clasped in his frozen fingers, and

his arms hung at his sides like lead weights. Yakorix fixed him with a yellow-eyed stare of hate, and from her balcony above, Kensa let out a gleeful laugh.

"Kill him now, Yakorix!" she cried.

As Tom glanced towards the witch, he saw a flicker of movement in the doorway far below the balcony where she stood.

He felt a rush of relief. It was Elenna! She had managed to put on her cloak, and was dragging herself along the icy ground. The sheer bravery his friend was showing filled Tom with new strength. *I won't let her down!* he vowed.

He turned his head and locked eyes with Yakorix. The Beast dropped

down onto all fours, and Tom saw
a terrible fury burning deep in her
yellow eyes. He raced forwards and
leapt, swinging his sword towards
the dark spikes that ran down her
spine, many already blunted by
his blade in the earlier skirmish.
Suddenly, her huge paw swiped out.

BAM! Tom found himself lying on
the floor halfway across the room, his
ears ringing and his jaw throbbing
with pain.

"Ha ha!" Kensa let out a whoop of
joy, and Tom saw Elenna wince.

He pushed himself up and turned
to face the Beast again, putting his
numb fingers to the red jewel in
his belt. Immediately he felt waves
of rage and hate pulsing towards

him from Yakorix – her whole being seemed to be filled with fury.

Why are you doing this? Tom asked her. *What do you want?*

Yakorix's lips curled back in a snarl, showing her curved, yellow teeth. Her voice in Tom's mind was a hateful growl. *I want what is mine. I want what was taken from me. The North is mine. Even the Icy Plains that the weakling Nanook claims to protect. I will take it all. The Witch has promised me this.*

Tom shook his head, speaking aloud: "Kensa wants the whole kingdom for herself. Whatever she has promised you, she can't be trusted."

Yakorix glared at him for a long

moment, and Tom waited, wondering what was going on in the animal's mind behind her yellow eyes. He glanced at Kensa, and saw a flicker of worry cross her smooth brow. Then Yakorix slammed her huge forepaw down onto the ice, making the chamber shudder.

I don't care about that! she said. *I am Yakorix, ruler of the North. Avantia deserves everything it gets for exiling me!* The Beast's body suddenly stiffened. She stood with her head tilted to one side, eyes narrowed. Then she lifted her snout and sniffed the air. Her eyes flashed with hungry satisfaction and she turned towards Elenna, who was lying shivering and helpless in the

doorway. Tom felt a shudder of
horror run through his body as the
Beast's voice echoed in his mind.

*And that punishment starts with
the death of your friend...*

6

FIGHTING FOR TIME

Elenna's eyes went wide with fear as Yakorix charged towards her.

No, you don't! Tom engaged the power of his golden boots and leapt onto the Beast's broad shoulders, grabbing a handful of matted fur. Then he drew back his shield and slammed it hard into the side of Yakorix's head.

Yakorix shook her muzzle and let out an angry snarl. Her head whipped around, and her long yellow teeth slashed towards Tom's face. Tom slid from the bear's back onto the hard ice as the Beast's teeth snapped together, closing on empty space.

He heard a strange crackling sound from above him. He looked up to see Kensa touching the tip of her staff to the amber jewel at her throat. Then she turned the staff on Tom.

A bolt of golden lightning shot from the tip. As Tom dived out of the way, the energy bolt struck the ice where he had been standing. *She's combining the amulet's magical heat with the energy of the staff.* The ice hissed and melted, leaving a mushy crater in the floor. Tom scrambled to his feet and glanced at Elenna, hunched and shuddering in the doorway. She locked eyes with him momentarily, then looked pointedly towards Kensa, who was holding her staff to the jewel at her throat once again. Tom understood Elenna's unspoken message, and nodded.

The jewel is the key to defeating the Witch.

Yakorix let out a growl and snatched for Elenna with her front paws. At the same moment, Tom leapt and slashed his sword. The blade bit into spikes, and Yakorix roared with rage, spinning away from Elenna to face the new attack.

Tom called on his golden chainmail, which lent him strength of heart. *I have to go on.*

Yakorix padded towards him. Her paw lashed forwards powerfully. Tom met the Beast's blow with the tip of his sword, driving it deep into the flesh of her paw-pad. Yakorix roared and drew back her paw forcefully, spattering droplets of blood across the ice. The crimson liquid froze where it fell, and Yakorix staggered away from Tom with a throaty rumble of anger and pain.

"Finish the boy!" Kensa screamed, her voice edged with fear. The witch was leaning over the balcony, her green eyes hungry and keen as she watched Yakorix. The Ice Bear's roars had faded to weak grunts now, each angry breath sending up a puff of white mist. The blood from her paw was dripping onto the ice, making a scarlet pool.

"End it for me now!" Kensa yelled, her eyes flashing with fury. Tom smiled. Behind Kensa, he could see that Elenna had climbed the steps and was reaching towards the Witch's neck. Elenna grabbed the chain around Kensa's throat and tugged. Kensa spun. When she saw the jewel dangling from Elenna's fingers, the

Witch screeched. But Elenna twisted her body and swung her leg, sending the flat of her foot hard into Kensa's chest. The witch fell backwards, crashing into the railings of the balcony. They shattered under her

weight, and Kensa toppled, clutching at the air as she plummeted to the ground.

Thud! She landed heavily on her back and lay gasping.

"Tom!" Elenna cried, lifting her arm and sending Kensa's jewel spinning

through the air towards him. Tom swung his sword…

Crack! As the blade hit the bright crystal, it exploded in a burst of golden light. Tom felt a wave of warmth rush past him, like the wind on a hot summer's day. As the golden

light spread outwards, the walls of
the palace shook and the chandelier
above rattled, as if the palace had
been hit by an earthquake. When the
light had faded and Tom could see
again, he found that the air around
him had lots its bite. The cold was
gone, and the walls were running
with water.

The palace is melting! he realised.

"No!" Kensa cried. She scrambled
up from where she had fallen and fled
across the room, slipping and sliding
on the ice as she raced for the door.
As she reached the arched entrance
to the room, she turned back to the
Beast. "Kill him!" she told Yakorix,
then hurried away. Yakorix was
sniffing the air and glancing around

at the glistening water dripping off the walls. But at Kensa's words, the Beast's gaze snapped back towards Tom. She bounded forwards, snarling and snapping with her jaws. Tom staggered back out of reach, hitting a column of ice behind him. Cold meltwater flowing off the column ran down the back of his neck, and the whole structure creaked ominously under his weight.

The sound gave Tom an idea. He touched the red stone in his belt. *Yakorix*, Tom told the Beast, meeting her glowing yellow gaze. *If you want to kill me you had better do it now. Your palace is crumbling. This is your last chance.*

EVIL NEVER RESTS

Yakorix let out a furious roar that shook the palace, making spatters of melting ice rain down from the ceiling. *You think you have won*, her voice echoed in Tom's mind. *But you will die!* The Beast's pointed claws flashed towards Tom. He leapt aside, and her blow connected with the ice pillar, sending a shudder through the room. Yakorix swiped again,

and Tom danced out of reach, faster
now that the biting cold was gone.
Yakorix leapt towards him, swinging
her paws left and right as if Tom
was a fly, but he ducked and spun.
The great Beast tried to reach him,
pummelling at the air and smashing
chunks of ice from more pillars in
her rage.

"Yakorix!" Elenna shouted, from
her place high on the balcony. As the
Beast glanced up at her, Tom took
the chance that Elenna had given
him. He lifted his sword and sprang
forwards, slicing his blade across the
back of Yakorix's knee.

Yakorix lurched, almost losing her
balance.

With the Beast distracted, Tom

looked up to Elenna. "Catch!" he cried, tossing his shield to her. His friend snatched it from the air and then leapt off the balcony, using Arcta's eagle feather to glide safely to the ground – while Tom lunged forward to slash at Yakorix's flank.

The Beast screamed in pain, the sound ripping through the air and echoing off the walls as the Ice Bear toppled forwards like a felled tree.

CRASH! Yakorix's massive body ploughed through another column of ice. Tom dived clear, rolling across the floor as the column began to collapse.

The noise was tremendous. Yakorix's arms flailed as huge chunks of ice masonry smashed

down, burying her struggling body.
Slabs of ice from the ceiling fell too,
smashing and skittering across the
melting floor. A great shudder ran
through the ground. Tom scrambled
to his feet to see shafts of sunlight

pouring through the ceiling, and
glittering drops of water raining
down, forming dancing rainbows.

"Tom! Run!" Elenna cried. "The
palace is collapsing!" Eerie groans
and creaks echoed all around them.
Another pillar of ice collapsed,
sending up a spray of water.

A figure hobbled into sight, framed
by the icy entranceway of the palace.
Kensa! The Witch's face twitched
with rage as she surveyed the water
pouring down the walls and the
bright holes forming in the ice. She
turned to Tom, her lips quivering, and
shook her staff.

"Don't think you've beaten me!" she
cried. "I'll be back. And your victory
will be a hollow one. You might have

defeated Yakorix, but now you'll have to spend the rest of your sorry days knowing you sent your beloved Nanook to her doom! I commanded my Ice Marauders to finish her." Kensa turned and streaked back out of the palace, her wet hair sticking to her face and the hem of her sodden dress floating in the floodwater.

"We must help Nanook!" Elenna exclaimed.

Tom and Elenna broke into a run, splashing through the water after Kensa. The long, winding corridor was flooding fast. Soon the water almost reached their knees. It was bitterly cold, and buffeted against them, making it impossible to run, so they both dived forwards and swam.

Tom powered his arms through the water and kicked hard, fighting against the freezing torrent. At last he could see bright daylight ahead. He burst from the flooded corridor and out into the entrance hall, then scrambled to his feet. Elenna fell to the floor beside him and he pulled her to her feet. Water was pouring

across the floor all around them and cascading down the melting ice-steps. Tom and Elenna half ran, half skidded towards the steps, dodging huge slabs of falling ice masonry on the way.

When they reached the courtyard outside, they could see the ice there was melting, too. The great moat that ran around the palace was filling up, the water as high as Nanook's waist. Her upper body was covered with half a dozen Ice Marauders, all clinging to her fur and hacking at her with shining weapons. Tom could see bloody gashes on the Good Beast's arms where the creatures' knives had cut her, but her blue eyes were bright and her movements were swift as she battered the monsters with her fists.

"Get off her!" Elenna set an arrow to her bow, and let it fly over the Ice Marauders' heads. It hit the wall of the chasm with a thud. The marauders stopped hacking at Nanook, and all looked up, glancing about for the source of the shot. When the creatures' chilly gazes settled on Tom and Elenna, Tom lifted his sword.

"Leave Nanook alone!" he shouted. "Can't you see that you've lost? It's over."

The Ice Marauders let out a chorus of howls and chuckles, chattering their spiky teeth and

waving their knives at Tom. As
soon as the creatures loosened
their grip, Nanook roared and
shook her massive body. The Ice
Marauders flew from her fur and
splashed into the moat. They started

paddling with their long arms,
but the current was strong. The
water swirled the monsters around,
tugging them under, then spewing
them back to the surface. Tom could
see the struggling goblins' arms and
legs becoming more transparent as
they started melting. The hollows
of their eyes and mouths gaped
wider. Soon their flailing arms were
as skinny as twigs, and their faces
were barely recognisable. Not long
after that, they were gone.

Tom heard Elenna let out a shaky
breath of relief as she gazed down
into the water. "I hope I never see
another one of those things again,"
she said.

Tom nodded. "Me too." He pointed

towards the palace drawbridge, which was almost completely melted through. "I'm afraid you'll have to climb onto my back again," he said.

Elenna shrugged. "I supposed I'm used to it now," she said. "But it's not very dignified!" She hopped up onto Tom's back. He engaged the power of his golden boots to leap across the moat, just as Nanook heaved herself out of the water.

Tom landed beside the Beast, then hastily set Elenna down and lifted his shield – just in time to deflect the rain of icy droplets that filled the air as Nanook shook her coat. Laughing, Tom lowered his shield and touched the red jewel in his belt.

Nanook looked back at him, her

blue eyes shining. *Yakorix sleeps once more*, she said. *Spring is coming.*

Tom smiled. Already he could see the sky clearing. The grey clouds were burning away, revealing the vivid blue above them, and the sun was high and bright. "King Hugo will be very relieved to hear it," he said. Then he glanced across the Icy Plains and his smile faltered. *I just wish we'd caught up with Kensa...*

As if in answer to Tom's thought, a great shadow fell across the snow. Tom looked up to see the black silhouette of Sanpao's flying pirate ship sailing over their heads towards the volcano. As it passed the tip of the mountain, Tom saw a

long rope snake down from the side of the ship, and a slim form wearing a trailing dress quickly shimmy up.

"Kensa," Elenna said, squinting up at the ship. "So she and Sanpao are friends again? In that case I'm guessing it won't be long before they think up something else to keep us busy."

Tom nodded, gazing after the retreating ship. He turned south. Throughout the kingdom, the winter would be thawing without Yakorix's magic. The frozen ground would soften and farmers' livestock could graze again. Food would be plentiful for King Hugo and Queen Aroha's people.

"Evil never rests," he said, as he trudged the first steps on their long journey back. "But neither shall we."

CONGRATULATIONS, YOU HAVE COMPLETED THIS QUEST!

At the end of each chapter you were awarded a special gold coin.
The QUEST in this book was worth an amazing 14 coins.

Look at the Beast Quest totem picture inside the back cover of this book to see how far you've come in your journey to become

MASTER OF THE BEASTS.

The more books you read,
the more coins you will collect!

Do you want your own
Beast Quest Totem?

1. Cut out and collect the coin below
2. Go to the Beast Quest website
3. Download and print out your totem
4. Add your coin to the totem
www.beastquest.co.uk/totem

Have you read the latest series of Beast Quest? Read on for a sneak peek at STYRO THE SNAPPING BRUTE!

CHAPTER ONE

AN UNEXPECTED WELCOME

"It's just up yonder," the coachman said, lifting a hand to point. His sleeve fell back, revealing a hairy, muscled forearm and the edge of a blue-black stain. *A tattoo?* Tom's stomach clenched as he noticed the jagged teeth of a reptilian skull at the base of the mark – the mark of the Pirate King, Sanpao. Tom ducked back into the carriage, his pulse racing. *He's a pirate!*

"Tom!" Elenna clutched his arm and pointed through her window out to sea. A bulky shape was sailing towards them across the sky, casting a dark shadow onto the waves below. It had a curved hull and billowing sails, and at the top of its foremast, a Beast-skull flag fluttered in the wind.

Sanpao's flying ship!

Read STYRO THE SNAPPING BRUTE to find out more!

FIGHT THE BEASTS,
FEAR THE MAGIC

Are you a BEAST QUEST mega fan?
Do you want to know about all the latest news,
competitions and books before anyone else?

Then join our Quest Club!

Visit the BEAST QUEST website
and sign up today!

www.beastquest.co.uk

Discover the new Beast Quest mobile game from

Available free on iOS and Android

Guide Tom on his Quest to free the Good Beasts
of Avantia from Malvel's evil spells.

Battle the Beasts, defeat the minions,
unearth the secrets and collect
rewards as you journey through the
Kingdom of Avantia.

31901060181924

DOWNLOAD THE APP TO BEGIN
THE ADVENTURE NOW!